Perseverance

THE TORTOISE AND THE HARE

Adapted by Carolyn Quattrocki

Illustrated by Tim Ellis

Copyright © 2000 Publications International, Ltd.
ISBN: 0-7853-4305-9
Leap Frog is a trademark of Publications International, Ltd.

Once upon a time, in a great forest, there lived a hare and a tortoise. Tortoise was slow with everything he did. He sometimes ate his breakfast so slowly that it was almost time for lunch before he had finished. He kept his house very clean and neat, but he did it at his own pace—very slowly.

Hare, on the other hand, was quick as a wink in all that he did. He would be up in the morning, finished with his breakfast, and going for an early walk in the forest before Tortoise had gotten out of bed. Hare could not imagine how Tortoise could stand to be so slow all the time.

Tortoise lived next door to his good friend, Squirrel. Squirrel had a cozy little home high up in an old oak tree. She loved to spend her time scurrying around. Squirrel, like Hare, wondered how Tortoise could always be so slow.

Hare lived near his old friend, Owl, who was not nearly as quick as Hare. In fact, he spent a lot of his time sleeping. But Owl was a very wise and good neighbor. Sometimes he thought to himself, "Hare always seems to be rushing somewhere in a hurry. I wonder if he ever slows down?"

"What are you doing today, Owl?" yelled Hare as he ran by Owl's tree house.

"Oh, hello, Hare. I'm napping as usual," replied Owl. "Where are you off to in such a hurry?"

"I'm very busy. I have to run around the lake," said Hare. "Then I must hop over some logs, across some large puddles, and over some bushes. Then I'm due for some short sprints through the forest."

"Good for you, Hare," said Owl, closing his eyes again. "Have a good time."

"Thank you," called Hare. "I will!"

Every afternoon, when the weather was nice, Tortoise would gather up his paints and brushes and go out into the woods. Tortoise loved to paint pictures of all the flowers, the trees, and the stream near his house. He worked slowly, but his pictures were very beautiful.

"Every stroke of my brush must be done carefully," said Tortoise to himself.

Tortoise took a lot of time choosing which paints he would use to paint a picture. Sometimes half a day would go by before he decided which shade of green to use on the leaf of a violet flower. Then another day would go by as Tortoise mixed the perfect color to paint the petals of the violet.

"Purple is the hardest color to make," said Tortoise. "Sometimes there is just too much blue or too much red."

Hare thought painting a picture was not at all exciting. "What a dull fellow Tortoise is!" Hare said. "Purple is purple!"

One day, Tortoise was sitting beside the road painting a picture of the pretty wildflowers he saw in the forest. Hare came up and said, "You are such a slowpoke. You've been working on the same picture all week!"

"I'm not slow," protested Tortoise.

"Silly fellow," said Hare. "You're so slow that I could beat you at anything you can name. Just name something, and I'll win."

"All right," said Tortoise. "How about a race?"

What an idea! Hare laughed and laughed at the thought of running a race with Tortoise. Hare laughed so hard he thought that he would explode!

"Great!" laughed Hare. "I'd gladly race you, Tortoise!"

"Fine," said Tortoise. "Then a race it is." As he said this, he turned slowly back to his painting. He went back to concentrating on painting the pretty wildflowers just right. He would worry about the race when the proper time came.

Hare was a little surprised that Tortoise did not seem afraid. He walked off toward home before he burst into his usual run.

Word of the race spread quickly through the forest. All the animals were talking about how Tortoise had boldly challenged Hare. "What was Tortoise thinking? Why did he do such a thing?" they wondered. "Did Tortoise really think that he could run faster than Hare?"

On the day of the big race, all the animals gathered at the starting line. Fox was to be the judge. "If the race is close, I will say who is the winner," he declared.

"Don't worry," said Hare. "You won't have a problem. I will be so far ahead, there will be no doubt about who is the winner of the race!"

Hare did a few quick sprints to show off for the crowd. Then he did some fancy stretches. Tortoise just jogged slowly in place.

"I don't want to pull a muscle," said Tortoise.

Tortoise and Hare stepped up to the starting line. Then Fox shouted, "Get ready. Get set. GO!"

The race was on! Hare dashed across the starting line. In the blink of an eye, he ran over the first hill, while Tortoise was just beginning to climb it.

"Slow and steady. Slow and steady," said Tortoise over and over to himself.

Hare was no longer in sight. Tortoise tried not to think about where Hare was. He just wanted to finish the race. He could do it, he thought.

"Slow and steady," Tortoise said.

Hare ran and ran until he was sure he would win. "This isn't even a race," he said to himself. "I think I'll lie down and rest a bit. Then I'll finish and still have plenty of time to spare. There's no way that slowpoke will ever catch up with me!"

So Hare stopped running, lay down under a shady tree, and soon fell fast asleep.

While Hare was fast asleep, Tortoise caught up to him. Then Tortoise passed Hare! Hare did not even move a hair as Tortoise jogged by him.

Suddenly Hare awoke with a start. "What was that?" he cried. He could hear cheering. He leaped to his feet and began running as fast as his long legs would carry him. But when he saw the finish line of the race, he could not believe his eyes.

Tortoise was almost at the finish line! He was about to win the race. Hare could not believe it. As he ran faster and faster, he could see Tortoise was crossing the finish line in front of him!

The crowd cheered and cheered. They ran to the finish line to congratulate Tortoise. Owl blinked his eyes and said what all the other animals were thinking, "Slow and steady wins the race!"

And indeed it did!

Perseverance

Perseverance means never giving up. Early in the race, it would have been easy for Tortoise to quit, because Hare was winning by so much. Even though no one thought Tortoise had a chance of winning, he kept going. Tortoise showed the other animals that anything is possible with a little perseverance.

As you grow, you will learn that things do not always come easily. Sometimes we have to work a little harder to be good at something. But as Tortoise shows us, wonderful things can happen when you do not give up.